For Rob, Sue and Chloe

First published in 2011 by Child's Play (International) Ltd
Ashworth Road, Bridgemead, Swindon SN5 7YD UK

Published in USA by Child's Play Inc
250 Minot Avenue, Auburn, Maine 04210

Distributed in Australia by Child's Play Australia Pty Ltd
Unit 10/20 Narabang Way
Belrose, NSW 2085

ISBN 978-1-84643-416-7
L041012CPL01134167

Printed and bound in Heshan, China

3 5 7 9 10 8 6 4 2

A catalogue record of this book is available from the British Library

www.childs-play.com

# The Lost Stars

Hannah Cumming

The world is a bright, busy place, full of noise.

The lights are always on.
People are always talking and moving.

They switch things on and they watch things and they do things, night and day.

They are so busy, that often they forget to stop and look up.

Every night, the stars come out
and go to work in the sky.

They are beautiful to see, and proud
to shine in the sky every night.

But they are getting fed up.

The light and the smog stop people from seeing the stars.

The stars have had enough.

They are taking a break.

In the meantime, the world is getting busier.

More and more lights go on...

...suddenly...

The power runs out.
Everyone is in the dark!

I remember years ago, there were bright things in the sky.

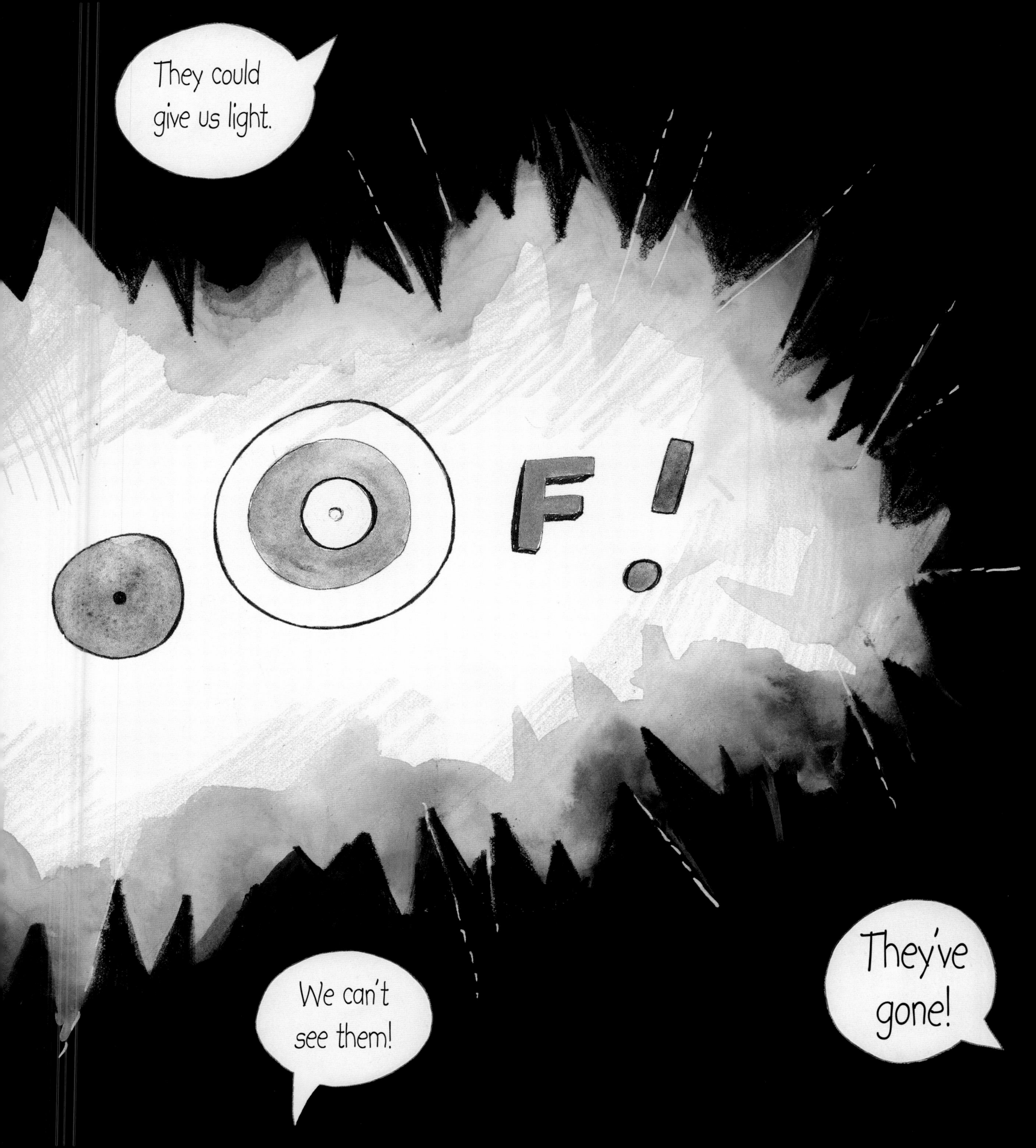
They could give us light.
OOF!
We can't see them!
They've gone!

A few remember the light of the stars.

They set off to track them down.

They search everywhere.

Sometimes, they think they have found the stars.

But it's not really them.

Finally, far away, they come across a beach.

Could it be?

They have found the lost stars! They beg them
to come back, but the stars are not sure.

Finally, the stars agree, but only if people promise not to forget them again.

The stars had missed the night sky,
and all of the people, too.

Everyone made sure that they would never
forget to look up at night again!